TM

A Book by Hasbro Bradley, Inc.
Pawtucket, Rhode Island 02861

Book
designed by Dick Codor and Pegi Goodman.
Written by Douglas Hutchinson.
Illustrated by Pat Paris

Eleroo's™
Big Surprise

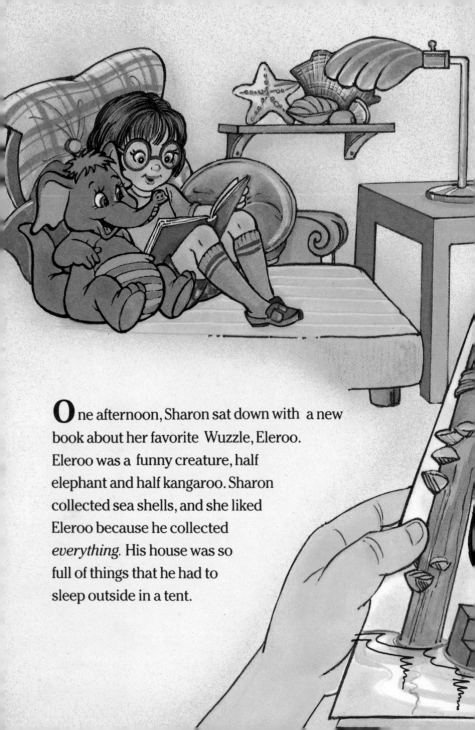

One afternoon, Sharon sat down with a new book about her favorite Wuzzle, Eleroo. Eleroo was a funny creature, half elephant and half kangaroo. Sharon collected sea shells, and she liked Eleroo because he collected *everything.* His house was so full of things that he had to sleep outside in a tent.

She began to read how one day Moosel was
puttering around in his shop when Eleroo came hopping
in. He seemed very upset and that wasn't like Eleroo at all.
"Moosel," said Eleroo, "I'm glad I found you. You've got
to help me. Something terrible has happened!"

Moosel put down his tools.
"Of course I'll help, Eleroo. What's the matter?"
"It's just the worst thing! You know that big raffle?
Well, I won!"
Moosel scratched his head in puzzlement.
"Why is that bad?"
Eleroo flopped down on Moosel's inner
tube chair, "You don't understand!
I need my raffle ticket to claim my
prize. And I've lost it!"

Moosel patted Eleroo's
shoulder kindly. "Now, now. I'll be glad to
help you find it. Do you know where you lost it?"
"Well, yes. It's in my house somewhere."
Moosel gulped. Eleroo's house was crammed to the
rafters with his collections. They'd never
find anything lost in there!

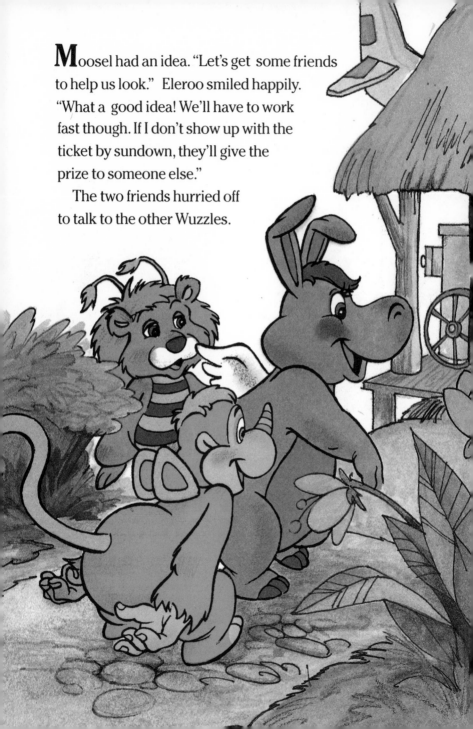

Moosel had an idea. "Let's get some friends
to help us look." Eleroo smiled happily.
"What a good idea! We'll have to work
fast though. If I don't show up with the
ticket by sundown, they'll give the
prize to someone else."

The two friends hurried off
to talk to the other Wuzzles.

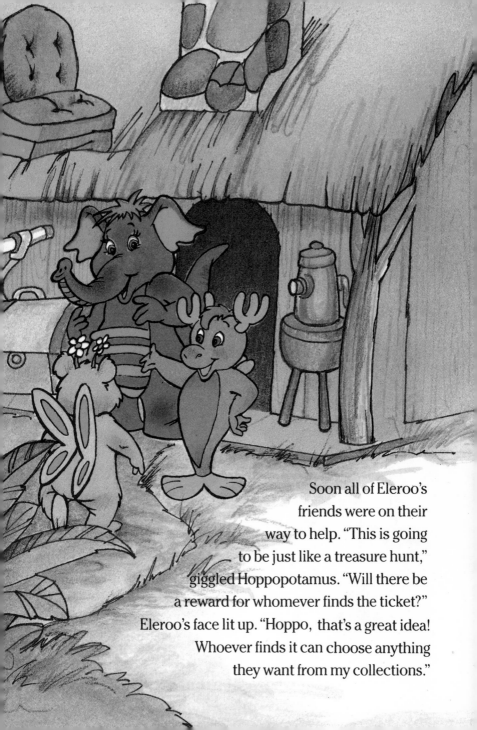

Soon all of Eleroo's
friends were on their
way to help. "This is going
to be just like a treasure hunt,"
giggled Hoppopotamus. "Will there be
a reward for whomever finds the ticket?"
Eleroo's face lit up. "Hoppo, that's a great idea!
Whoever finds it can choose anything
they want from my collections."

When they walked into Eleroo's house,
Butterbear looked around her in dismay. "Gosh, I
knew Eleroo had a lot of stuff, but I'd forgotten how *much!*
This will take forever!" However, Bumblelion always saw the
sunny side of things. "If we get right to work, I'm
sure we'll find it in no time."

Everybody started
looking in his own special way.
Moosel made a careful map of the rooms.
Then he divided them into numbered areas so
he could search more efficiently.
Rhinokey hung from the
chandelier and checked
the stacks of things
from the top.

Bumblelion just started digging into the
stack in front of him, tossing things every which way.
Butterbear tunneled underneath, in case the ticket had fallen
under something. And Hoppopotamus went
to the kitchen to look for some food.

Bumblelion picked up a broken tennis-guitar.
"Eleroo, you should get rid of some of
this stuff. Things like this are just useless."
"That's not useless," Eleroo protested. "Suppose I
find a big ball of tennis-guitar string. Wouldn't I
feel silly if I'd just thrown that away?"

Moosel held up half of a broken flower pot-clock. "How about this? Why are you saving it?" "Oh, I couldn't throw that away. It's part of a collection!" Moosel frowned, "How many of these have you collected?" "That's the only one so far. Don't forget, whoever finds the ticket gets to choose a prize," Eleroo reminded them. "Have you all chosen something?"

Everyone had. Bumblelion liked a fine old stopwatch- baseball bat.

Hoppopotamus picked a pretty thermometer-vase,

and Rhinokey admired a lamp shade-hat that looked particularly good on him.

After several hours of poking
and pawing through the mountains of
junk, everyone was getting tired and grumpy.
Rhinokey began teasing Butterbear by spinning old
plastic dish-pillows at her. Butterbear growled, "That's not
funny!" They almost got into a fight until Bumblelion
quickly changed the subject. "Eleroo, you never
told us. What's the big prize you won?"

To everyone's surprise, Eleroo seemed
embarrassed by the question.
"Oh, gosh, this is silly, but I don't
remember. Er, say, you know I
think I might have put that
ticket in the garage. I'm
going to go look."
And he dashed
outside.

Bumblelion scratched his
head. "He's acting very strangely. He must
remember what the prize is. An Eleroo never forgets."
Hoppopotamus snorted angrily. "I think he's just being
selfish. He's afraid he'll have to share his
prize with us, so he's pretending
he doesn't know what it is!"

Just then a stack of newspapers tipped over on
Hoppopotamus! She wasn't hurt, but it made her very angry.
"I've had enough of this! We're never going to find that ticket! I'm
going home!" Everyone agreed and they all walked out.
Poor Eleroo, standing outside, heard what Hoppo said.
The ticket was still lost, and now all his friends
were mad at him! He felt terrible!

Sharon felt very sorry for Eleroo. "Oh, I wish I could be there to help Eleroo! I wish, I wish, I wish I was in the Land of Wuz!"

A tear trickled down her cheek and landed on the book. Suddenly there was a flash of light, and Sharon couldn't believe her eyes! Because she was there, right there in Eleroo's house!

Eleroo jumped in surprise. "My goodness!
Who are you?" "My name is Sharon. I'm a
friend. I know all about you and your trouble
with the raffle ticket. And I want to help if I can."

Eleroo smiled gratefully. "Thank you,
Sharon. Can you start digging through
that pile? It's almost sunset."

Eleroo turned to the nearest pile of junk and started tearing through it, tossing things every which way. "I know it's here somewhere, and I've got to find it! I've just got to!" Sharon tried to calm him down. "Maybe there's an easier way. I always thought an Eleroo never forgets." Eleroo stopped and looked at her. "Well, I don't."

"Think back, when you bought the ticket, where did you put it?"

Eleroo thought hard. "I remember putting it in my pouch."

"And do you remember taking it out?" Sharon asked.

"Well—no!" He reached into his pouch, searched around a bit . . .

and, with a gasp, pulled out the missing raffle ticket!

"**Y**ou found it!" shouted Sharon. "Oh, Eleroo, good for you!" Eleroo nodded sheepishly, "I never forget. But this time I guess I didn't remember to remember. And look at all the trouble I caused. I have an idea how to make it up to my friends. But I'll need your help." And he told her what they were going to do.

A little later that
evening, Hoppopotamus was
relaxing in a nice mud bath when a
note was slipped under her front door.
It said, "Please come to Chez Wuzzle for
dinner at 8:00 tonight." Chez Wuzzle was the
fanciest restaurant in the Land of Wuz! She got
all excited, quickly dressed and raced out the door.

When she got to the restaurant, she couldn't believe her eyes. Eleroo sat at a table with all their friends. And each friend had been given the prize they chose from Eleroo's collection. He smiled at her. "The raffle prize was this dinner. That's why I couldn't tell you what it was. I wanted it to be a surprise!"

Hoppopotamus felt very ashamed of herself. "I'm sorry I walked out on you. How did you ever find the ticket in time?"

"I never could have done it without the help of my good friend Sharon," he said. Sharon felt so happy she thought she would burst. So she gave Eleroo a big snuzzle as everyone cheered!